Dear Parents:

Congratulations! Your child is taking the first steps on an exciting journey. The destination? Independent reading!

STEP INTO READING® will help your child get there. The program offers five steps to reading success. Each step includes fun stories and colorful art or photographs. In addition to original fiction and books with favorite characters, there are Step into Reading Non-Fiction Readers, Phonics Readers and Boxed Sets, Sticker Readers, and Comic Readers—a complete literacy program with something to interest every child.

Learning to Read, Step by Step!

Ready to Read   Preschool–Kindergarten
• big type and easy words • rhyme and rhythm • picture clues
For children who know the alphabet and are eager to begin reading.

Reading with Help   Preschool–Grade 1
• basic vocabulary • short sentences • simple stories
For children who recognize familiar words and sound out new words with help.

Reading on Your Own   Grades 1–3
• engaging characters • easy-to-follow plots • popular topics
For children who are ready to read on their own.

Reading Paragraphs   Grades 2–3
• challenging vocabulary • short paragraphs • exciting stories
For newly independent readers who read simple sentences with confidence.

Ready for Chapters   Grades 2–4
• chapters • longer paragraphs • full-color art
For children who want to take the plunge into chapter books but still like colorful pictures.

STEP INTO READING® is designed to give every child a successful reading experience. The grade levels are only guides; children will progress through the steps at their own speed, developing confidence in their reading. The F&P Text Level on the back cover serves as another tool to help you choose the right book for your child.

Remember, a lifetime love of reading starts with a single step!

Visit us on the Web!
StepIntoReading.com
rhcbooks.com

Educators and librarians, for a variety of teaching tools, visit us at RHTeachersLibrarians.com

Library of Congress Cataloging-in-Publication Data is available upon request.
ISBN 978-0-593-18207-9 (trade) — ISBN 978-0-593-18208-6 (lib. bdg.) —
ISBN 978-0-593-18209-3 (ebook)

Printed in the United States of America
10 9 8 7 6 5 4 3 2 1

This book has been officially leveled by using the F&P Text Level Gradient™ Leveling System.

JOHN CENA
ELBOW GREASE

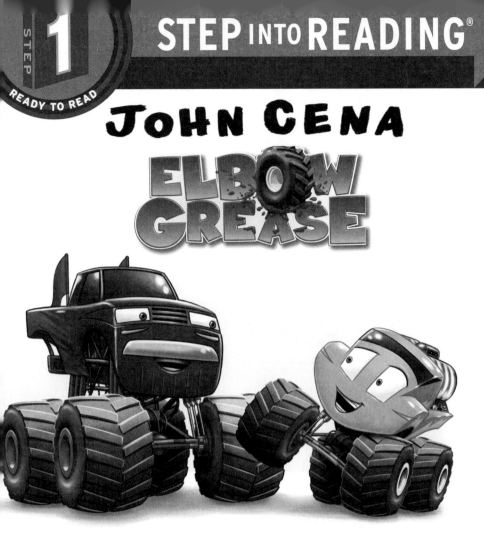

DRIVING SCHOOL

Cover illustrated by Howard McWilliam

Interior illustrated by Dave Aikins

Random House 🏠 New York

Elbow Grease

is a

monster truck.

VROOM!

He loves to race
with his brothers.
It makes him happy!

But today,
Elbow Grease is upset.

Pinball is ready to learn.
So are Flash, Tank, and
Crash!

Come on!

Elbow Grease is
just sleepy.

The trucks meet
their teacher,
Big Wheels McGee.

Time to hit the track!
The trucks go fast
and kick up dust.

WHOOSH!

Elbow Grease goes
too slow.

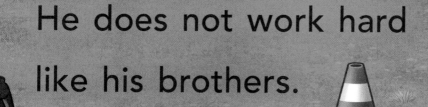

Pick it up, 'Bo!

He does not work hard like his brothers.

21

Before long,
his brothers
get stronger.

Wait up!

They jump higher
and go faster.

Elbow Grease
never gives up.
He starts to
work harder.

Soon, Elbow Grease

can go faster

and jump higher, too!

Now he knows
his brothers were right.

Driving
school
is cool!